MURDER: ABOVE TOP SECRET

by:

J.L. " Jim" Hodges, Lead Investigator

TABLE OF CONTENTS

Foreward

Fewer than 1% of the general population of Earth understand intelligence work and even fewer have experience in any form with the underworld. The operators who learn, adapt, and live in this realm are carefully chosen, rigorously trained, and submit to practice-to-polish daily innovation and exercises of network building and psychological warfare. In the early days of one better-known agency, the CIA, young men were predominantly surreptitiously recruited from the Civil Air Patrol as flying skills were highly regarded, and the military type orchestration of their young and open minds was modeling clay for the masters of their craft to shape, mold, and perfect. The profession of intelligence work is a craft which is compared to magic, in that the object is to fool the audience into firmly believing that an action seen with their own eyes is always real. The true master never allows anyone but their chosen assistants to look behind the curtain.

In this story of fiction based on the true story of murder and mystery, you will be introduced to some of this master craft in action. Take the personal challenge as you read, and try to identify some of the puzzle pieces included. You may just help solve a cold case murder, *Above Top Secret*!

Introduction

A gruesome torture style murder had taken place of a top-level electronic warfare developer, contracted to the United States federal government for the ultra - top-secret, Strategic Defense Initiative, AKA, "SDI", and also known as, "Star Wars Defense Initiative", a set of M.I.C. (Military Industrial Complex) war-tech, *killer* satellites. You will not read about this case in any book or newspaper, nor will you find it online.

The case you will learn about is the real torture, and murder of Donald Charles Neil, however some of the names and locations have been changed to protect this case for prosecution of any future suspects that may be brought to trial. Also to protect witnesses, and informants, as well as contract intelligence sources still working within networks, to preserve evidentiary rules, and fit publication clearances. It was opened as a homicide case, on June 07, 1983, in the City of Webster, Texas and is still an active murder case, and continues as an active investigation at the highest levels of secrecy.

I was the lead investigator of this case from the original dispatch call, and today stand as the only frontline witness to the entire investigation. Though other officers performed in support roles, they were never fully briefed, nor was my partner and supervisor at that time, Detective Sergeant Jerry Barker, who is now deceased.

Some records were removed, redacted, and destroyed by unknown sources, both during the case investigation and subsequently. The*, **Above Top Secret** designation, was placed several years earlier, actually before the call of the murder came into the Webster Police dispatcher in 1983.

I never give up on a case, and after all these years, I am compelled to bring this forward as a cold case, and deploy the highest technologies now existing, and work through both current, and former law enforcement and intelligence resources to try to solve the case and seek prosecution.

As you read, keep in mind the fact that the swollen and wax putrified body at the crime scene was never officially identified, and the exhumation order was denied by the judge.

Herein, you will be briefed on some facts, puzzles, general evidence, as well as operational speak, on our covert journey to see if this murder - **Above Top Secret**, can be solved.

Prelude to Murder

The *Above Top Secret* project was rolled out directly from the Office of the President of the United States on a, *need to know* basis. Don Neil was the only one briefed as a contract intelligence operator and consultant on feasibility on an unknown date in 1981. However, this project was not even known among intelligence agencies, or discussed within channels until March 23, 1983 – shortly before this murder took place. The very hint of this operation becoming reality sent shock waves through the intelligence communities in every nation in the world, as the desperate race for the final frontier of military domination – space - was in high gear, and the smallest ripple made a tidal wave of speculation, and fear through all governments. Each knowing that control of the orbits around Earth would give superior tactical dominance. This role was essential for the United States, as they had already dominated the land, sea, and air within the atmosphere – space was the ultimate prize, and they could not lose this contest, and the other governments of the world could not allow them to achieve it.

The President addressed the nation on March 23, 1983:

Historical Intelligence Briefing: The President of the United States, Ronald Reagan

ADDRESS TO THE NATION ON DEFENSE AND NATIONAL SECURITY

March 23, 1983, Key Points

My fellow Americans, thank you for sharing your time with me tonight.

America does possess -- now -- the technologies to attain very significant improvements in the effectiveness of our conventional, non-nuclear forces. Proceeding boldly with these new technologies, we can significantly reduce any incentive that the Soviet Union may have to threaten attack against the United States or its allies.

As we pursue our goal of defensive technologies, we recognize that our allies rely upon our strategic offensive power to deter attacks against them. Their vital interests and ours are inextricably linked. Their safety and ours are one. And no change in technology can or will alter that reality. We must and shall continue to honor our commitments.

I clearly recognize that defensive systems have limitations and raise certain problems and ambiguities. If paired with offensive systems, they can be viewed as fostering an aggressive policy, and no one wants that. But with these considerations firmly in mind, I call upon the scientific community in our country, those who gave us nuclear weapons, to turn their great talents now to the cause of mankind and world peace, to give us the means of rendering these nuclear weapons impotent and obsolete.

Tonight, consistent with our obligations of the ABM treaty and recognizing the need for closer consultation with our allies, I'm taking an important first step. I am directing a comprehensive and intensive effort to define a long-term research and development program to begin to achieve our ultimate goal of eliminating the threat posed by strategic nuclear missiles. This could pave the way for arms control measures to eliminate the weapons themselves. We seek neither military superiority nor political advantage. Our only purpose -- one all people share -- is to search for ways to reduce the danger of nuclear war.

My fellow Americans, tonight we're launching an effort which holds the promise of changing the course of human history. There will be risks, and results take time. But I believe we can do it. As we cross this threshold, I ask for your prayers and your support.

Thank you, good night, and God bless you.

President Reagan delivers the speech on March 23, 1983. Oval Office.

Geographic / Intelligence Briefing: The Bay Area, 1983

Mainstream spies, covert operators, and big money of international influence ran thick in the small communities surrounding the Johnson Space Center, known to locals as the Bay Area, but this story centers on the unassuming small City of Webster, Texas, also known as the "Gateway to the Bay Area", which skirted Houston, Texas sprawl. Deceivingly, Webster, Texas was a small community that only encompassed approximately 6.6 miles in 1983, and had a real population of roughly 2,200 residents, but a daily transient population of almost a quarter-million. The 1960 - 1970 census, and records explained Webster's significance, indicating a boom of 578% population because of the NASA project, and expansion – thus, its' gateway, designation. The original Nasa Road One ran East, and West, right through the center, and was crisscrossed at the city's center by Texas State Highway 3, and a parallel railroad track.

Roy Johnson, well into his golden years, ran the City of Webster as its' mayor with an iron fist, commonly pounding the same into desktops, or striking his walking cane sharply against the floor, and yelling, "...By God, Nasa Road One was a cattle trail when I got here – and by God, it will be cattle trail until I die!!". Roped by blazing passions of the right way, and the wrong way – or, more truly stated: The Johnson way, and no way at all - Roy

Johnson wielded his cane, shook his fist, and stood tall, and fast on his bowed legs – the perfect alter ego of Don Quixote - while prosecuting the business of the city. However, he was a dream gift to the hardcore international covert types, steadily infiltrating his defunct utopian cattle empire. It was here, that hard-shell members of violent groups began to infiltrate this sleepy, quiet, and hardworking community in the period of 1978. These groups included many heavyweight underworld figures, the Mafia, and a host of puppet felons, pumping drugs, domestic violence, and general unrest through the pipeline of the Bay Area as unknowing co-conspirators in a cover for true espionage, and big money M.I.C. types.

There was a sense of urgency in the air, as cloak and dagger operators of all crafts, from all corners of the globe, were descending upon the Bay Area to ramp up existing operations and upgrade *shop* for some long-term spying, and counter-spying operations, generally on some advanced technologies which were being drafted, and proposed in the NASA communities. However, in 1981, there came a whisper in the wind, directly from the office of President Ronald Reagan. It was the most ominous proposal of high flying satellite technology to ever be uttered and speculated against the enemies of the United States of America – the S.D.I. projects. In the world's knowledge banks are some unsettling facts for our enemies to digest: The United States of America has been dominant on the land, sea, and air defenses since WWII. The last frontier will be space, itself, and if SDI projects were fulfilled, it would mean complete checkmate of power within the human experience.

The City of Webster Police Department had a colorful history as well, and some widespread reputations, which garnered heavy community scrutiny. The school zone, which spanned Nasa Road One for roughly a mile, was well lit with flashing yellow lights across the street on both the entrances, and exits both ways, 20 miles an hour speed limit signs every 100 feet, a Webster Police Officer working traffic on foot at a cross street intersection, and plenty of traffic radar enforcement officers that aggressively wrote books of tickets each school day.

To help reform the department, a new Chief of Police was announced, who had grown up in Webster, was promoted from within. He began adding officers with integrity to the department, however, Mayor Johnson still beat the drum for increased revenue, via traffic tickets, and class "C" misdemeanor arrests, so that the money stayed in the city coffers.

My closest friend joined the department in 1977 and later went on to retire as a lieutenant with 22 years of service. I followed him, joining the department in February 1978, and rose quickly from patrol officer to detective. It was in this assignment that I would excel, tapping on my experience, and expertise.

I had been unknowingly recruited by a close family friend, Jack Blaine, and U.S. intelligence services as a covert contract operator in 1967 while I was in Civil Air Patrol, and learned the value of, H.U.M.I.N.T (Human Intelligence) building a mass network of informants, and channeling craft through controllers, and peers, to perfect a real craft at, "Magic". My controller, Jack Blaine, was a WWII, and Korean War veteran, and was a partner in forming the C.I.A., although not mainstream. As a contractor, he took control of many covert assignments and was a true *magician,* who was an active international player, mainly in Cuba, Mexico, South America, and the Persian Gulf. I would soon learn after joining C.A.P. that he was a friend of my father in WWII, and they met and worked together on multiple projects in, and around Arak, Iran. Jack was also a close friend of Galon Moseby our next-door neighbor and was very active flying with the C.A.P. I began to put these puzzle pieces together as Jack and Galon Moseby were pilots, engineers, and electronics wizards, just like my father. Very soon after we moved to Baytown, Texas, my father began to fly as well. Jack was in shadow with me after I enlisted in the United States Army, and as I quickly rose to the rank of sergeant, fought as a combat infantryman in Vietnam, as well as other places, both during, and after active military duties. We continued to run operations through my experiences in professional security, law enforcement, intelligence, and a myriad of businesses.

I was approached by the commander of a newly formed federal task force in the later 1970s, to help them with the Vietnamese shrimpers, and the U.S. shrimpers as an advisor during what has been coined, "The Alamo Bay Incident", which a subsequent movie was made about. It was during this operation that my street network became priceless, as I knew about things before they happened, and knew the operators, and the punks they employed, as well as the streams of money, and bad actors that were surreptitiously combing the back doors for any information about S.D.I.

I am writing the majority of this briefing from memory, as unknown agents disguised as FBI agents removed the majority of the case files and certain items of physical evidence from the City of Webster Police Department illegally. Due to the size of the combined volume of the evidence, this required the use of a bobtail truck similar to that of a mid-sized rental moving van. The theft of this evidence occurred after I left employment with the City of Webster, and before my former partner, Jerry Barker became ill and subsequently died. I only discovered the evidence theft on July 1, 2015, when I returned to the Webster Police Department to gain access to the case files and evidence, in hope that some of the blood evidence could be used for DNA and to copy notes for this briefing. The new Chief of Police was not aware of this case and was as surprised as I was when the missing evidence was revealed. The chief instructed the records manager that there were files missing and she checked again but found nothing more. This photo illustrates what I was given as the complete file, and is all that exists of the case as of July 1, 2015.

(Redactions Noted)

Jerry Barker was promoted to Chief of Police a short while after my departure, and served as such during the time that unknown agents, disguised as FBI Agents, contacted him about removing the evidence so that the FBI could follow up on the case. These were imposters who illegally removed key pieces of the evidence by deception. I talked with other officers of the Webster Police Department who remembered seeing them talking to Chief Barker. They described them as wearing dark suits and showed FBI credentials. They utilized a moving truck and dollies as described, to remove files, computers, and other pieces of evidence.

There were a few leads that caused this case to be reopened periodically after I left the department, however, Barker never contacted me or spoke to me again regarding this investigation. He pulled away from the investigation while it was underway and began to avoid discussing or helping at all. Barker also avoided any contact with me after I left, and though I called numerous times over the years to inquire about any new developments he never returned my phone calls.   This will be detailed later within the briefing.

Profile Briefing on Victim: Donald Charles Neil

Donald Charles Neil was born in Bradford, Pennsylvania on May 13, 1930, and he was 53 years old at the time of his murder. His older brother, that we will call, Reginald herein, described that Don Neil was very intelligent and studious which caused social problems. His brother further stated that Don did not have any friends and developed a wicked temper. Don Neil left home after high school and kept very secret about his life events following, other than his marriage and birth of one daughter by that marriage. This photo is from Don Neil's current security and intelligence clearance badges of 1983 which I located at the murder scene. I have kept the number found and what agencies, clearances, and other information secret to protect key facts of the case.

(Redactions Noted)

I did contact his wife (Location and name withheld) during this investigation and found that they had been divorced for many years and that she had remarried. I will describe more about their marriage and other facts related further on in this briefing. She added that Don Neil had worked for Bell Helicopters for 28 years as an electronic warfare design engineer. According to her, Neil had worked on the laser sighting devices for the Cobra gunship, early computing devices, and many other projects which he could not divulge to her. She described that he had later begun traveling to meetings and was changing jobs to work for a NASA contract firm. She described that his older brother had talked with Don

Neil as he became more withdrawn and secretive and simply advised his brother that he had taken on a very top-secret project which paid very well. Both his ex-wife and his brother stated that this was extremely important to Don Neil, as he wanted his daughter to be proud of him, and he was also trying to gain custody of her ever since the divorce.

Don Neil had moved into a large apartment complex which was located at 515, and 535 Nasa Road One in Webster, Texas in 1978. Neil moved into an upstairs apartment at 535, which is marked as # 210-A as of July 1, 2015. According to all evidence at the scene of the murder, he had disconnected the heat and air conditioning and lived as a recluse in complete filth and piles of magazines and electronics parts ever since he took up residence there. He always told the apartment managers that he did not want anyone entering his apartment as he had allergies, and did not like to be bothered.

His brother advised me that in a phone conversation with Don after he moved into the stated apartment that he was just playing with satellites, and other top-secret projects, and never spoke much about it.

It was during these operations, and investigations that several spies were identified, and tracking had begun. They were from the old U.S.S.R., and China, and there was the threat of counter-espionage by agents of various U.S. intelligence, law enforcement, and military agencies, as well as rouge contract operators, and M.I.C. mercenaries.

All good spies loved this time period, as it was before the advent of wide-spread home computers, cell phones, biometrics, DNA, high process fingerprint computers, dash cams, etc. The social pressure had not begun on driving while intoxicated, and clubs stayed full almost every night of the week with revelers hanging around to close the joints at 2:00 am, and then going to breakfast at restaurants that they knew illegally served after-hours coffee with various liquors applied. In the Bay Area, there were clubs, swelling with movers, and shakers everywhere. This allowed for the surreptitious chatter to flow freely from loose lips, and filibusters alike. The people who worked on NASA projects were under very high pressure and had some known hangouts where they pooled immediately after work. One of these was very well known as the U Joint – it was called, Fort Terry as well. Though nothing more than a shotgun wood-framed building full of NASA autographs, and various photos of missions past, it was packed with high-pressure types that would regularly start fights and trouble. It was an infiltrator's dream.

The general streets were tough, and two apartment complexes seemed to be the launchpad for most of the calls for service. One was at 800 West Nasa Road One, and the other occupied both, 515, and 535 West Nasa Road One. The names have changed many times over the years, but there was always a joke around the Bay Area that any applicant to either complex had to have a felony record to be accepted as a resident....it was no joke! The murder of Don Neil took place at 535 West Nasa Road One, apartment 210-A, which was upstairs, and faced the courtyard close to the management office. The scene and location will be described in other parts of this report.

Chapter One: 608 is Dispatched

June 7, 1983, started as a beautiful and very hot day in the city of Webster Texas. My partner and I, Sergeant Jerry Barker, had stopped for breakfast at the Days Inn Hotel restaurant at 1001 W. NASA Road One.

Photo of the old Days Inn as it stands in 2019. The restaurant was through the middle set of front doors on the left-hand side.

In those days, this was the local gathering point for law enforcement officers to eat and get coffee from various agencies. Joining us was my very close friend and colleague, Deputy John Eckhoff of the Harris County Sheriff's Office. John and I had worked on many secret, as well as business projects together for many years. We had just finished the last arrests and paperwork from a very long federal taskforce investigation and were enjoying the quiet and peace at hand. We had a few sips of coffee and a few bites of our food when I heard the police dispatcher call, "608", which was my badge and radio number, over my handheld radio. I noted the time at 9:52 am, as I acknowledged the call. The dispatcher informed me that the apartment manager at 535 West NASA Road One had entered an apartment on a welfare check and smelled a foul odor and noted that the apartment was in horrible condition. She also advised that patrol officers were requesting us to come to the scene as they believed the smell was coming from a putrefied body inside the apartment but the manager could not see into the apartment. Sergeant Barker and I left our food and headed that way with Deputy Echoff following to check by with us.

It was only a short drive straight up Nasa Road One, of roughly a half-mile from the Days Inn to the scene, and we all arrived at 9:58 am. This would be a day that would live with us for the rest of our lives.

As we pulled up into the circle driveway by the apartment office we noticed a Webster Volunteer Fire Department truck and City of Webster police cars already on the scene. There were several civilians standing around talking in small groups. The immediate, and a very familiar strong odor of a dead body was overwhelming at approximately 150 feet from Neil's apartment, and Sergeant Barker and I looked at each other with shock knowing that this day was going to get really long – really quickly. Scanning the area, l noticed several of my confidential informants were scattered at various locations, and I purposely avoided them to preserve their anonymity. Webster Police Officer J.T. Smith met me and began the briefing. I asked him quickly if there was anyone in jeopardy and he stated that he had not heard of anyone injured at this time.

Photo: Circle Driveway 2019. Upon arrival, we parked where the white van is pictured here. The murder scene is on the second-floor apartments at the far end, running left to right.

Officer Smith stated that he had received a welfare call from the dispatcher and checked by with the apartment manager, who I will call Sally (actual name withheld) for this report. Sally had informed Officer Smith that she received a call from someone claiming to be the employer of one of their residents, Don Neil, and was concerned as he had not come to work or called in several days. Sally stated to Officer Smith that she and her assistant manager went to Don Neil's apartment and began smelling a horrible odor. They knocked on Neil's door but got no answer. Sally further stated that she called the maintenance man, who I will call Ken (actual name withheld) for this report, on their hand-held radio and asked him to come to the apartment. Sally continued by stating that while the maintenance man was on his way, she continued to knock and call Neil's name out, but no answer. I then met with Sally and her assistant as well as the maintenance man, who had just walked up to where we were talking. All of them were visibly shaken and had been throwing up at the horror of what they had seen and smelled upon opening the door to Neil's apartment.

Sally continued by stating that when the maintenance man had joined them at the door of Neil's apartment, he advised them that he had checked as he was on the way, and found that Neil's station wagon was parked in its' assigned parking space. Sally stated that she asked Ken to open the door to Neil's apartment as this was very strange. Ken stated that the door was unlocked so that he didn't have to use a master key to enter. Sally stated that as they opened the door and entered, they were sickened by the smell and trash piled high to the ceilings, and there were no lights on in the apartment. For a bright sunny day, it was very dark in the apartment. We would later assess that this was due to the mass of clutter, as well as the thick brown mold that had developed on every wall in the apartment, transforming the walls from white to dark brown in color. Sally stated that they called out

Neil's name as they began to enter, but they had to walk on this very narrow pathway lined with stacks of electronics magazines, and parts stacked all the way to the ceilings and scattered into the kitchen area, where they observed stacks of unfinished plates of food and maggots overtaking the entire area.

Sally stated that they peered into the bedroom and could not see anything except computers, electronic devices, parts, and wires were strewn about, and mixed with piles of clothing which covered the entire floor. The only other room was a small bathroom which was also cluttered with clothes and electronics parts and wires. Nobody or the person was found. Sally further stated that they left quickly as the air temperature was over 100 degrees inside, and they were getting sick, and in fact, threw up after leaving. Sally stated that she then called the Webster Police and asked for an officer to check by.

Photo: Apartment 210-A is on the second floor where the small barbecue grill is located in the photo.

Officer Smith stated that he arrived and met with Sally and the others, who related the same story to him. Officer Smith stated that he had entered the apartment, but just made a quick look around and left after finding no one, and nobody. I asked Officer Smith to coordinate with the other officers on the scene and begin interviewing witnesses, while Sergeant Barker and I checked the apartment again. I asked Deputy Echoff to personally interview a resident who was retired and lived in the courtyard, who was a confidential informant for me. I thought assuredly that she would have seen, or heard something. I knew that Deputy Echoff knew how to conduct himself so as not to give her status away.

Chapter Two: The Initial Crime Scene

I had seen a lot of horrors and crime scenes, but this one was hauntingly eerie, macabre and unusually strange. I entered first with Sergeant Barker, I adjusted myself as I walked through the same narrow pathway going into the living room. Sally and her team were with me. The heat in the apartment was unbearable, and the stench of death, that I know all too well, was overwhelming, stinging our eyes and arms. I noticed that there was another short pathway to my right-hand side, which led to a chair and a lamp area where we would determine later that Don Neil would come home, turn to the right and sit in the chair, turn on the lamp, and either read the publications scattered around, or examine and assemble electronic parts.

I then went to the kitchen, where the maggots were crawling over everything. I could not walk into the kitchen due to cluttered old food half-eaten, pots and pans and more magazines and electronic parts scattered all over the floor, counters, sink, and cabinets.

Moving into the short hallway, I began to notice that the once white painted sheetrock walls were now brown from the mold. The darkness in the room was only brightened slightly by the Sun shining through the rear window of the apartment. Other than this, there was no light available due to the normal light switches not working. The hallway was only a few feet long and heavily cluttered with more magazines, electronic schematics, and technical papers stacked to the ceilings. I also noted here that the thermostat had been long removed and spider webs were thick over the exposed electrical box.

I then entered the only bedroom and to my left but straight ahead, I saw a pair of dress slacks hanging from the doorknob of the bathroom door which was opened into the bedroom area. A pile of assorted clothes lay heaped in the middle of the floor, with an ironing board set up in the middle of the pile. I immediately noticed an oscilloscope partially sticking out of the clothing with what appeared to be a good amount of blood on it. Computers and electrical parts lined the back wall on two tables, and to my right were three tables filled with computers, monitors, electronic devices, and cables of all types running around the room. There was also a large closet to the right filled with the same type of equipment. After passing across the threshold and into the bedroom, I noticed the carpet was soggy and my snakeskin boots became soggy.

One anomaly noted was a strange-looking device stuck on the rear window glass that covered one pane and had a round, thick black electrical wire attached that went to one of the computers. The object appeared to be a flat piece of plastic-wrapped with black electrical tape with a large bulge about the size of my closed fist, which housed an electrical box. This was stuck to the pane with some type of glue, as we could not free it later.

It was apparent that whoever lived there was using the living room as a research area, and the bedroom as a laboratory for computer and electrical work. No bed or other furniture was present except for the single chair mentioned in the living room.

There was no person or body visible which left me and Sergeant Barker stumped. I concluded that perhaps the trash and mold were bad enough to create the smell and that the occupant had left for work, left town, or if there was a crime scene, the body had been moved. As we stood there silently looking around, I noticed a human hand, which was in full wax putrification, sticking up out of the clothes pile in the center of the floor. The fingers had already melted away and the skin had an opaque white appearance. I pointed to the hand and more closely visually examined the clothes pile again.

I realized that the watery substance that I was standing in was leaked body fluids from a dead body, directly at my feet. It was then presumed that a red wool blanket was wrapped around the head of the victim, and other clothes had been piled on top to conceal the remainder. I immediately thought of two possibilities directly related to my training. It is very common for a suspect to cover the victim, especially the face if they know the victim intimately and don't want to look at what they've done. Secondly, I drifted back to my covert days and remembered in our training a method to enhance and accelerate the decomposition of a body to make identification difficult, or impossible. My mind began to swim in experience, training, and critical thinking – flashing backward and to the present in rapid pulses. I wanted to be exact and leave this investigation knowing I had exhausted every skill and degree of luck that I could muster. I felt that I always owed that to the victim and their loved ones. I also owed it to the people, who had placed their trust in me as a police investigator.

I drew a diagram at that time with my sketch pad to indicate the floorplan and what we had found. Realizing that we at least had blood on the oscilloscope, the hand of a deceased person, and watery fluid in the carpet, I asked Sergeant Barker to retrieve my camera so that we could begin photographing our progress from thereon. Also, as Ken had stated that he found the front door to be unlocked, there could be a known suspect that we needed to identify and apprehend quickly. I asked Officer Smith to begin photographing all of the on-lookers, as sometimes the suspect will be at the scene to examine the process for various reasons.

Sergeant Barker and I exited the apartment for a short period to get our eyes cleared out, get some fresh air, and speak to a few of the officers and witnesses before returning and continuing our investigation. I asked the fire department if they would stand by as we may need oxygen and some protective clothing, and they agreed.

While officers at the scene continued to interview witnesses, Sergeant Barker and I focused on the best way to process the crime scene. After borrowing some bunker boots from the fire department I bagged my soaked boots and marked them as evidence for later examination. Sergeant Barker and I plotted our strategy and we reentered the apartment. I carefully photographed my way in, and directly to the bedroom. Once there I set the camera down, and Sergeant Barker and I moved some of the clothing which exposed a putrified and bloated body that was stuck to the clothes with seepage coming from the swollen and bloated condition of the body.

We could see that this was a male who was positioned on his back wearing blue and white print boxer shorts. I began to photograph every discovery as we went and Sergeant Barker assisted with logging photos and items for evidence. As we removed more excess clothing from on top of the body, we could see that the deceased had no pants on but still had black socks on, up to mid-calf.

He was also wearing a white dress shirt that was still buttoned up and had a pocket protector with writing pens and mechanical pencils in the top left-hand pocket. As we removed the clothing his body began to purge and the tightened skin slipped from his abdomen and began to spew slightly. The last item, which was the red blanket that we now could clearly see, was wrapped tightly around his head.

Sergeant Barker and I both had to manage this as it was tightly wound and almost glued in place with wet and dried body fluid. As we lifted the blanket free, his face was stuck to the blanket and came off with some of the rear portions of the scalp and some hair. The body fluids really spewed from his mouth, nose, and eye areas. I photographed the removal, and we logged more notes as I began to sketch out exhibit numbers. Sergeant Barker and I examined the full-body now and made notes that the body appeared to be a stocky built white male, possibly of middle age as the hair that was visible was salt and pepper colored.

The deceased was lying on his back almost in the middle of the bedroom with his head closer to the bathroom and arranged horizontally to the back wall of the apartment. We realized right away that an autopsy was going to be mandatory and identification was going to be really tough as the face was essentially melted and not recognizable or able to be reconstructed. I examined his hands for fingerprints and noted the left hand, which was the one I noted initially sticking straight up in the air was too badly decomposed for any prints, and the right hand was withered and black at the fingertips from decay.

I did my best to photograph the process as I retrieved smeared fingerprints from three out of five fingers of the right hand. This was extremely difficult due to the conditions, and the position of the body. I logged those as evidence on my sketch pad. We could not determine a cause of death as the body was too decomposed and covered with smeared stains of body fluid mixed with blood, however, we both suspected a homicide due to the blanket wrapped around the head.

Sergeant Barker and I went back outside to get some fresh air and try to get cooled off a bit. I instructed one of the officers to notify the Harris County Medical Examiner's Office so that they could come and declare the person we found as dead, and make arrangements for the autopsy and transport. We entered the room again to finish what we had started. It was a long day of smell, anger, and panic and since we were police officers, it is our job not to show all of these.

I checked with the officers on the scene but there were no witnesses that related anything unusual. Deputy Echoff did find that one of my informants had some detailed information, and he motioned me to her apartment. This lady, that I will call Erma herein, was in her late 80's at the time and called me regularly to give information on suspicious things going on within the courtyards and grounds of the apartments. I always feared for her safety but she was a strong-minded and tough lady who was not fearful of the residents or their friends.

On many past occasions she gave me credible and reliable information, so what she had to say would be valuable. Erma related that she had watched Mr. Neil carefully as she felt sorry for him living alone, and she was bothered by some of his activities. She stated that she had witnessed a Hispanic female who appeared to be approximately 5'2" tall and medium build in her 20's entered Neil's apartment at various times of the day, and on several occasions, none of which constituted a pattern, and none of which correlated in proximity to his death. She described these visits as being sporadic and spread over several years.

She further stated that she had witnessed a white male approximately 5'8" tall and medium build who appeared to be approximately 30 years old with curly blonde hair and light blonde mustache wearing blue jeans and t-shirt enter Neil's apartment on June 3rd, at approximately 5:30 pm. Erma stated that she had never seen him before and did not know how long he was there. Erma further recalled that none of them ever knocked, or used a key, they just entered by opening the door.

I thanked Erma for her information and asked if she would give a written statement to Deputy Eckhoff, which she agreed to and submitted within that day. Deputy Echoff took her to the Webster Police Station and had her statement notarized after completion. I left Erma's apartment and briefed other officers on the scene so that they could investigate these leads while interviewing other witnesses. I then returned to follow up on the crime scene.

I met up with Sergeant Barker and briefed him on the interview with Erma, and we prepared for continuing our crime scene investigation. Patricia Coldwell had arrived from the Harris County M.E.'s Office at 11:14 am and was waiting for us by the firetrucks in the circle driveway. Sergeant Barker and I were putting on fire boots and getting a few hits of oxygen before re-entering the crime scene. Mrs. Coldwell asked us if there was a body and I explained what we knew so far, and told her that we already had numerous photos of the crime scene and the body.

She stated that she would fill out the appropriate death certificate and officially pronounce the person dead. I explained that we assumed that the body was that of Donald Charles Neil, but we were not completely sure as no formal identification had been made, or was possible conventionally. I requested a special autopsy be performed including swabs for semen and blood testing with me present. Mrs. Coldwell wrote these on the request sheet she was working on. She never entered the crime scene, however, she did ask if I would take some photos for her on her camera, which I did and returned it to her.

Sergeant Barker and I re-entered the crime scene. We went back inside to have the deceased packed and to be taken for further examination.

Note: Dictation Begins to Lada Andropov, Transcriber

Carrying a decomposed body is always a nightmare. It was steady at first, trying to lift the swollen body until Sergeant Barker tried to lift it by hands instead of by the shoulder and then the unimaginable puff of the horrible smell of petrifying decay. We managed to wrestle the body into a body bag and off it went to autopsy still leaving all the terrible smell of decay for us to bear like a cross.

The room spoke to us the language of evidence and we knew that the more we look, the more we see things that may help us if we must solve the case. We went digging up the mysteries of papers lying across the room like a thick carpet. We were certain that something was somewhere in the room and as the smell reduced with time, our energy for searching through intensified formidably until we recovered the ID badges across the room under a pile of cloth that housed the biggest pile of maggots we saw in the room.

If there was a badge, then there was an external factor that contributed to the murder. I walked around the room gently, pretending that not so many activities were going on around me. I tried to imagine the scene afresh as though my memory could travel back in time to put images and persons at the right spot so that all I was seeing would make a complete sense. I was trying to solve a murder scene right on the spot but I could not.

If anything at all, everything I could ever imagine was entirely skeletal. I needed flesh and blood, emotions and sounds, fingerprints, everything that can help me recreate a perfect occurrence and every detective knew this is best done by gathering witnesses, and solid physical evidence. We had attempted to speak to some witnesses but they weren't speaking anything helpful. I walked out of the room and Sergeant Barker followed me. We decided to talk to neighbors that were close to the crime scene who, as a matter of layout, should hear, see, or feel, that something was not right on the day the crime was committed.

Neil, the man we assumed was the decomposed body, was a large man. A man that wouldn't die in such a state as we met him without a good fight. Putting up a good fight explains why there were lots of scattered paper and clothing all around the room. There were neighbors who lived directly above and below him aside from the good neighbor Erma. It was just as a matter of certainty that they should have heard something. I was preparing my mind for possible answers when I threw my question at them. I was prepared to hear excuses as flimsy as them saying they were listening to loud music or they were partying to the extent that they couldn't hear any form of violence going on.

Sergeant Barker started the investigation almost immediately, talking with the neighbors about anything they could remember. A lot of them gave the expected answer, 'we heard nothing'. Even though such an answer was as annoying as anything, it was too early to begin to press them too hard. We were ready to let them all be and definitely check on them later but we were left in a state of shock when we returned to find them stealthily moving out in twos and threes with no forwarding addresses and no notice to us.

It was one of the patrol officers that first noticed while we were talking to the last neighbor who was the only one to give us a meaningful clue. 'I could have sworn that I heard something disturbing at the parking lot some few nights ago but I wasn't really focusing so I didn't look', the fragile voice explained.

'What did you see?', I asked expectantly.

'I just said I didn't look. If I didn't look I couldn't have seen anything', the fragile voice replied to me almost wishing she hadn't said anything at all. I wasn't ready to push her to the limits so I had to let her go. That was the point my attention was drawn to some other neighbors who were moving out.

The balcony I was standing on with my partner gave a vivid view of them. Some of them were those we had already spoken to and we could see they were all afraid that similar things might happen to them. They all felt insecure and it was expected. Although it was expected, it was also dangerous.

'Go to the district Judge and ask them for an order to seal this apartment', that was all my head could think of and that was what I said. There was lots of evidence lying around and still untampered. The best way we can protect the scene was to make sure that no one could come in and tamper with the evidence. With the flow of people trying to leave and the possibility of people trying to satisfy their curiosity came the issue of tamper of evidence. Since we weren't a newbie in the game, we knew what to do.

It was almost dusk and the effort of so many hands was everywhere. News reporters had not shown up, which was odd as they all have police radio scanners, but our police officers were moving all over to carry out their different assignments. Even Neil, if he could see us, would smile at a job well done at the time. It was overwhelming and the overwhelming feeling was something that cannot be hidden.

Officers had been positioned on drive-by shifts. We got our order from the court and the apartment was completely sealed, leaving the police force to be in charge. It was much later at night while I was drinking my last cup of coffee that I knew how stressful the day had been and how if I must continue, I needed a lot of rest to push the investigation right where it needed to be. It was a slow drive home but I had the rain to comfort me as the wiper moved slowly across the windshield, revealing the long way home which I craved so much.

****

The night was long and sleep was so far from my home than I had expected. Having gone through a tedious and tiring day, I had expected that sleep would come quickly, but it didn't. I rolled in my bed until I had no choice but to stand up and walk to my bar. I had little whiskey left in the bottle and nightmares of the Vietnam War came to haunt me.

I could bring myself to take the final sip out of my glass of whiskey but memories of what had happened during the day came back to me overwhelmingly. I could picture the crime scene and how the decomposing corpse cried out for justice. I shrugged when I remembered how the corpse had burst open when we were trying to lift it up. It was a pathetic memory that I had witnessed many times before.

I shook off my head and walked back to my balcony. I tried to imagine what it must have been like on the balcony that night. I tried to imagine people walking by hearing the screams and loud noises but didn't care enough to give a call to the police. I tried to imagine the neighbors and what they could have been doing and then the scene of the bursting decomposing body came back again. I shrugged again and swallowed all the content of my cup in a gulp.

When I woke up, it was barely dawn. The loud ring of my telephone woke me up and as I tried to rush out of bed, I was restrained by the pounding ache in my head and I knew the next thing to do was to reach out for a cup of coffee. The coffee wasn't so hot but I needed to drink something in a hurry and get out of the house. My destination was clear. I had instructed the body to be taken for autopsy and I needed to follow up on it. By the manner of practice, I was supposed to be there for the autopsy to take place. I was supposed to monitor every step the medical examiner took in making sure the right samples were extracted to bring out nothing but the best results.

When I got there, it was a strange feeling. Unfortunately, men in dark suits who stated that they were from the funeral home had arrived during the previous evening and transferred the body into a metal transport casket.

'We were expecting you to be here for eight' The chief examiner stated when I walked up to him. He walked around with a hint of superiority tainted with haste that suggested that something was wrong.

'What about the body?' I asked him with a demeanor that suggested that I was strictly there for business and nothing else. He looked around and followed my gaze settling on a transfer paper with the funeral home listed in Bradford, Pennsylvania on it and a set of signatures, one of which was supposed to be Don Neil's brother.

'That's all I know...' He said while avoiding to maintain eye contact with me. He walked hastily into his office and I followed. As soon as we were both in, he shut the door and started his long conversation about how four men had come to him earlier all dressed in black. He could have sworn they were a member of the force even without them showing him any identity card or barge. He explained that they showed the paper for transport and were so much in a hurry to pick his body up.

He removed his glasses and wiped off his forehead with his handkerchief. I could see his trembling hands and everything happening was just a signal that something wasn't entirely right.

'Can you check by later? I am currently very busy to attend to you now sir!' The chief examiner said as he battled with forces only he knew and finally grabbed a seat to sit. He went on to remark about directing his subordinates to allow these men to pick up the body and ship it right to Bradford Pennsylvania.

'Did you run any test on him before he was taken away or do I need to have a federal judge's order before you can speak?' I said in a tone I couldn't really remember. He stopped trembling for a while, put his glasses back on and looked at me through it in a pause that lasted almost forever.

'Look, I don't know what to tell you but whatever happened to that man wasn't natural as you already know. He was murdered in cold blood and had to put up a good fight. The cuts on his body are markings from an unusual knife... I would have said more though if I had finished my examination. Look, I don't want any trouble, okay? Not anyone of the government'. I stood still trying to search through my mind to know where to start, but answers seemed to have eluded me. I saw him waving at me and pointing to the door and even though I felt like pressing him further, I knew he was already living in his own world of fear and nothing could save him from what his inner guilt was doing to him. I knew that I could order the autopsy later.

As I walked into the lobby of the hospital, I took a split second to stop and gather myself and find some logic with which to move forward. I looked around and I saw worried faces looking back at me with a plea that almost translated to me stopping what I was doing. I drove away seriously trying to piece a strategy together.

My vehicle's radio was picking up other calls when I got it cranked up. I had a thought then to call the funeral home to verify why they had come for the body so soon. There was a phone booth just across the road, and I fished out some quarters for the call. I dialed the phone number listed for the funeral home and talked with the receptionist.

'I am calling in regard to the newest body that was flown into you just a few hours back. There is still an ongoing investigation and I'd like to continue by inspecting the body a little more. Can you hold it until I can get a court order in your town? Can I check in later today?' I asked enthusiastically, awaiting nothing but a positive answer.

'So sorry, we just buried the body a couple of minutes ago! May I know your name and where you are calling from?' the gentle voice behind the other end of the line replied. I asked a lot of quick questions that she was not able to answer and suggested I talk to the director.

Chapter Three: Setting Up the Intelligence

Don Neil's apartment was my new office; I did all my paperwork there. My paperwork left a terrible replication of the mess that the room had been when we first walked in it except that this time, there was no strong decaying stench and the dead body to worry about. I didn't want to go home because I was trying to be as careful as possible. I wouldn't want to drag my private life or family into the messy investigation that was ongoing at the time, and I was beginning to sense that something very sinister was at play. I had seen these types of interrogations used before, whereupon the victim is accidentally, or purposely killed in the intensity of it. This appeared to me to be a technique widely known that is similar to waterboarding, the difference being that in this case suffocation was used, and a knife to torture the victim. This would make them believe that they were really going to die and they would spill secrets. I explained this to my partner, however, he had no experience with these things and wasn't able to offer much. I called Deputy Eckhoff to meet me as he did have covert experience.

Deputy Echoff met me at a safe house that was located at the King's Inn Hotel in Webster, Texas. John and I kicked the scenario around and agreed that we needed to call Jack Blaine for assistance with inside information.

- **Detailed maps of Istanbul Turkey had been found at the crime scene and many letters of correspondence with coded names and messages from Turkey. This was an operational area for Jack Blaine and my father during WWII and he helped establish CIA (Then, the O.S.S.) ties thereafter within the Persian Gulf region. I met with Jack at the Sheraton Kings Inn to go over the materials. Jack advised me during this meeting that his Washington D.C. FBI contacts had advised him** that they were working a very high-level shadow investigation and wanted to keep a low profile and hands-off appearance, though they would offer other resources of the intelligence community to keep themselves clean of involvement. Jack already knew John, Bob, and Darren (Introduced later), but also warned me of several KGB and Chinese agents posing as intel case officers as well as FBI agents to throw this investigation off. Ironically they were closely tied with Jack Blaine due to his work with Iranian Savak during the recent revolution. Jack advised that he had a valuable Iranian asset who used the name Hosain Mahmood Sutgar and was cleared high enough to cooperate and accept assignments. Jokingly, but seriously, Jack had advised that he was a chain smoker, and drank huge amounts of Arak Vodka, but seemed to work better somewhat intoxicated. He was working on some of the signal intelligence received regarding infiltrators combing info about SDI and those assigned to the project since 1980. He also advised that he enlisted another asset who was using the name Archie Fletcher, who had worked as a British Foreign Service Officer, and code specialist, and was now freelance. He had worked with Jack and my father on project Qum, a joint U.S. and British venture, and was forced to leave the U.S. Embassy there, also in 1980. They had learned that President Reagan had apparently chosen only Don Neil to attempt the SDI program to control tight security, and due to Neil's Wild West style of innovating strategic technologies. The security around this SDI development was astoundingly strict. "EYES ONLY"

I was certain that Neil left a relative and I began the arduous task of tracking them down. Maybe the relative had all the necessary information or maybe the relative didn't become a question. I was ready to settle after finding all existing relatives, friends, and colleagues.

Neil no longer had a public record that I could access to proffer answers to all my questions; a scenario that all pointed out how fishy his murder was. I was beginning to believe that he (Neil) was under the witness protection program, as we had numerous people living in the small cities surrounding Houston. I had gone back to the sealed crime scene to search through the piles of paper that were all strewn all over in the apartment. I coincidentally stepped on a picture of him smiling, beer in hand with a man that looked almost like him. I still remember the sigh of relief I made, knowing fully well that I had seen what I was looking for. Don Neil's brother.

He was a short man with a stern look, more sturdy looking than Neil was. He was polite on the phone when I talked to him about me coming to conduct an interview with him. Very hesitant at first but there was a voice in him that craved justice; a curious voice that wanted to express anger. I was going to tap into that to get further information, and possibly some leads.

When I got to his home, it was a modest home that had more flowers than I had expected. It was nothing like Neil's apartment. Reginald's home, as his name was, depicted that he had invested more effort in making sure he had a tidy home; something that showed that he lived quite a contrasting life when compared with that of his brother. Neil's life, as I began to see it, was almost very hasty. It was almost like he lived but there was nothing recorded about him not because he never really existed but because he seemed to always be on the run, and private. Jack Blaine and Archie traveled with me to the small town of Bradford, Pennsylvania.

'Welcome officers! What should I offer you, Coffee?' Reginald said as we walked in, cautiously before me, in a way that suggested that he was at the same time monitoring our every move. He wasn't sure whether to settle us in his sitting lounge or to take us into his living room. Cats were meowing almost everywhere in the house. I counted nine then I stopped.

'You don't like cats do you?' Reginald asked. I shook my head in a manner that wasn't specific and I told him I wanted water. On the wall of his home were more pictures of the family with Don Neil included. He wasn't smiling in any and he looked much younger than the decomposing body suggested. I gulped out of the large glass he gave me and cleared my throat to announce that we could start the business of the day. He walked to one of the many portraits of himself and Don on the wall, picked one up and walked back to sit down just opposite me.

'You know, we are just these two left in the whole world, aside from his daughter of course, and there was nothing Don wouldn't tell me. He had no friends just me...' He looked at me just at the point where I was trying to retrieve my pen from my pocket and I knew he wasn't interested in me writing anything down. This was a test of his preparedness and caution about his involvement. I signaled Archie to begin taping as he was wired. Jack wore the anti snoop rig and signaled to me after a few minutes that no bugs were detected. We were clear.

'I didn't welcome you into my home for you to quote me. I wanted to speak to you because maybe only you can help the world know the truth about his death'. He smiled as I accepted his water glass and settled into the soft sofa. He talked very little about his childhood with Neil which was very intentional. He attempted to tell me that he didn't want to get involved in any part of my investigation whatsoever. He didn't want to be part of this story as he didn't want his little world that exudes outward perfection to be tainted with whatever imperfection that might have ruined his brother. Reginald told us of his personal harassment, as he deemed it, by people from the government over the years due to his brother's assignments and dealings in the covert world. He explained further that "They" had sent female agents to seduce him into revelations about Don, as well as threatening men who followed him, and scared him and his family. He stated that he would also receive weird phone calls day or night. He was worn out with the whole process but did want passionately to find Don's murderer.

'He told me about a life insurance policy he was taking. It was a quarter a million in value and it was that point I knew that something was wrong. He said that he had named me his beneficiary and I felt something was just not adding up' Reginald finished his statement and opened the picture frame in his hand. I was startled because silence had descended upon us waiting for Reginald to volunteer more details. Instead, silently and almost reverently, Reginald removed the photo from the picture frame and stared at it for a long and uncomfortable moment.

'He said he was working on something, something really big this time and something he couldn't tell me more about that it was a satellite project blablabla...' He continued as though he had not planned the next step. Reginald stood up as to end the interview, threw the picture frame in the trash can, and tore out his face from the picture and gave the rest (Don's image) to me with a smile. He continued, explaining how he had watched the president's address about SDI and told Don it sounded like what he had described working on back in 1980. Reginald stated that Don confirmed that, and told him that the President had personally chosen him to design portions of the military items and laser guidance system for SDI. When pressed for more information Don told him that he needed to forget that he and Don had talked and that he couldn't talk anymore about it until it was declassified.

'I knew something was wrong but it wasn't my place to pester him so I let him be until this unfortunate thing happened ... do you need more water?'

'No... of course not. Please continue Reginald' I replied.

'There is nothing more to say actually. I am leaving it all for you to deal with but I know that his death didn't come naturally as you can already see. I can imagine the pain Don must have went through dying in such a lonely and horrible manner.' Reginald picked up one of his cats and tended it until I got his cue that it was time to leave.

Reginald may not have given so many details about the insurance policy but to validate his truth, I needed to make sure that policy was indeed executed. A good officer in the force may not be able to boast of so many things but a good network is essential for all officers and I could boast of it.

Getting the insurance company wasn't so much of an effort and confirming that indeed a quarter-million-dollar worth of insurance had been executed in favor of Reginald which made it almost natural to believe every other thing that he had said. The next thing for me was sharp in mind.

We returned to a Clear Lake safe house, and I began a sweep of Confidential informants (C.I.'s) that we had worked with for years and were good at their craft and well-recognized on the bar scene in the Bay Area. We were out in the clubs every night and worked with NASA types nearly every day as they all lived and worked around the Bay Area. For this investigation I put out just enough information and misinformation to balance the feedback that I received and sort out those who I needed in this investigation and those that were just combing for money, recognition, or the "get out of jail free card". I had more than twenty-five operators that I developed into CI's over the years, as well as 12 well-groomed assets, and they didn't disappoint this time. Sutgar proved his value at this point by cranking up the chatter in the clubs. He had forged I.D.'s, a solid assumed identity as an electronics engineer, and had the technical background that enabled him to talk the talk. I had more good information coming straight to me than I had ever experienced.

In almost all the links I was able to gather, it seemed that everyone was especially afraid of the three agents whose names we will say were, were John, Bob, and Darren (Previously mentioned). They were mature operators that I had worked around, and my contacts told me that they were no rookies, which is why they were picked for these assignments. True magicians of their craft.

I never made a close association with them or bled them for information as they strategically held themselves out as scientists and designers and did not associate with anyone who could not talk, "shop". It was apparent over the years that they were there, that they would not waste time on small talk. They were experienced and directed and worked as a tag team on certain NASA employees and contractors. They were certainly polished and professional – very straightforward. They had plenty of fake ID's and some in-depth technical backgrounds and were well-studied on the nature and weaknesses of the

NASA crowd. Jack and Archie were the perfect choices to shadow, and try to work into their confidence, using Sutgar as their bonafide.

John, Bob, and Darren had been circulating alcohol, women, and drugs, of a high-class nature, and paid bar tabs and arranged alibi's for more than one high profile figure laced with the community, even if they were from outside and traveled in – those expenses were covered as well. John was a fixed-wing and rotary (Helicopter) pilot and had been seen flying into Ellington Field (Now Ellington Airport) as well as Clover Field (Now the City of Pearland, Texas Municipal Airport), and Humphrey Airport (Now the City of Baytown, Texas Municipal Airport).

All of these were small airports with no traffic control, except for Ellington Field which sometimes had a controller during the daytime. After the Neil murder, I tried to find John's pilot certificates but there were no records by the name he was using.

During the high level covert federal task force operation I had begun working in 1980 with the Vietnamese shrimpers and the American shrimpers going to war with each other along the Texas Gulf Coast, I ran across them numerous times. What was strange is that this was the talk of the Bay Area and the Gulf Coast, and everyone from the KKK, to the Mafia, wanted in on the money to fan hatred and create a war between the two sides, however, these three never even hinted at it, or wanted anything to do with it. I knew then, that they were well-trained agents working something bigger than the shrimpers flare-up, but I couldn't find out who they worked for. I did, however, know what their mission was, and it had something to do with spying on our U.S. space program.

I used my training in disguise and transition to move around and keep tabs on common crooks as well as these types that were thick in the area. Deputy Echoff helped out as well, and although John was not a master of disguise, he was intellectually quick and physically challenging. He was a master motorcyclist which allowed a different look as we transitioned from one crowd to the next. I did get him a blonde and brown wig, two reversible jackets, a variety of ball caps, and three pairs of glasses which he learned how to use very quickly and effectively.

I had set up a few safe houses after serving on the shrimper flare-up federal task force beginning in 1980. I depended on trusted assets as well. One principal asset was J.W. Peterson who at the time was chief of security at the Sheraton Kings Inn which was located in the 1300 block of what was then, Nasa Road One (now renamed Nasa Parkway) in Webster, Texas. This was a large high-class hotel with a restaurant and bar which was a popular hangout for locals. J.W. had served in law enforcement before and allowed us to keep a few rooms for interviewing CI's and assets. Some had adjoining suites, or maintenance rooms, which allowed us to get informants in and out by various means without detection. There was also an elaborate camera system in the parking lot and inside the hotel.

I also called I.G. Blackman whom I hadn't seen in many years. He had served in the Vietnam War with me, and afterward in covert cross border operations in border towns along the Rio Grande. He also accompanied me for a very short soldier of fortune foray into Biafra and Rhodesia in the early 1970s during the range wars. His skills as a pilot and signal intelligence officer were unmatched. He was, fortunately, living in the North side of

Houston at the time and agreed to check in with us regarding cracking the codes on the computer discs found in Don Neil's apartment, examining the Hamm Radio transmissions and the mystery antennae, as well as bugging and tracking assistance on the ground. I thought that perhaps he could also assist with pilot information on our three contract agents.

He arrived in Webster and I made arrangments for him to use one of our safe houses as his "office". He went right to work with the rest of the team.

Another established hotel, the Holiday Inn, was right across the street from the Sheraton Kings Inn in the City of Nassau Bay, Texas, at the corner of then, 1300 Nasa Road One at the intersection of Space Park Drive. We also used this hotel in the same way. These were nice if we had picked up a tail on foot or in vehicles as we could lure them to the parking lots and record their vehicles, license plates and take photos of them as well. Both of these structures are no longer there. In addition to these hotels, we used airport hangars, boats and marinas, and restaurants as cover locations to carry on our clandestine work.

One outstanding safe house location where we set up I.G. and Sutgar should be specially noted on Telephone Road in Houston nicknamed, *Crack Row*. This was a mobile home park just a few miles from the Night Owl Club. I would like to give credit to one of my long-time CI's that made me a super cop through his covert work with me for over 16 years. Everyone simply called him Badgeman because of his twisted idealism of one day becoming a police detective. Badgeman was, unfortunately, a heavy drug user and went in and out of jail with his criminal cohorts for some heavy-duty crimes. He arranged for I.G. and Sutgar to get set up in the mobile home park and watched them day and night for protection. I will include Badgeman in a subsequent book, however, his affliction always caused him to admire me, and he was quoted more than once stating that he wished he could be just like me. He was always truthful with me and did not hide his problem with what he pontificated was, " A little man that stood on my shoulder who whispered bad things in my ear – things that I couldn't ignore". Badgeman was murdered in 1995. I always appreciated his loyalty, infectious smile,...and sometimes his humor. He was a dangerous man.

Chapter Four: Curious Mind

Donald Neil was a strange man and everybody had the same thing to say about him. He had lived in his apartment for over five years before the gruesome murder. In all of those five years, he had lived in a terrible condition which made the piles of papers, electronic gizmos, scribbles on scraps of paper very understandable.

'He never slept on a bed or mattress until his death. He slept on just bare floor' the maintenance guy said when I tried to ask him some questions. He went on to explain how he had all of his heating and air conditioning thermostats removed and insisted that no one should enter his room for cleaning and all of these were based on the reason that he had some sort of allergies. So many envelopes trashed from his room had so many unmatched names and suspicious codes and markings.

Matching new testimonies with the newly emerging facts was challenging and caused me to revisit the crime scene. The room had begun to take a different shape. The smell of rot had been replaced with a stale air of humidity. There were no red blood stains anymore, just a little bit of blackened spots with a handful of flies buzzing around them. I had all pieces of evidence that I had collected over time and I was determined to go through it one more time to find a missing clue if there was any.

I went through the pieces of evidence and photographed everything, tagging evidence such as a bloody oscilloscope, wallet of the victim found in his rear pants pocket with bloody right-hand index fingerprint on it, but no way to lift it or clarify it to be read. There were two small keys found in the wallet with 'N" marked on them that may have gone to safe deposit boxes but we could never find any, noted victim's suit coat and car keys were missing. Computers were found to have coded language and password protections, and I left them at the scene for development. No matchbooks, names, address books, etc. found. An odd device on the window hooked up to computers which were a blob of electrical tape over the electronic circuit board and device box that was glued to the top window pane of Neil's bedroom.

Neil was ahead of his time and designed this device and developed code to hit satellites much like space link technologies do today. Some newspapers and magazines were thrown away on the floor after scanning them for any notes or crime info. No murder weapon found even after getting every knife measured.

The next couple of days were once more spent in and out of the crime scene where I discovered and tagged new pieces of evidence. I wasn't alone this time, Sergeant Barker was there with me, searching and digging through facts with me until he discovered that not so long before Neil's death, he had reported a burglary into his storage shed. The attempt was rather specific according to the report on the case Barker found. It wasn't just a random ransack, the person who broke in targeted it like he knew what he was looking for. This brought about a new question in our minds. Why try to break into his storage shed? The more we looked into the question, the less wide the possibilities became.

We found a couple of other things. I found a name of an employee of the local Radio Shack in Neil's papers on a receipt for electronic parts and I went to talk to him about Neil. Unfortunately, He did not know Neil but did remember him buying things periodically. He also remembered other people coming in asking questions about Neil as if they were detectives but they never showed ID, just told him that they were checking up on his purchases from a credit card company.

'They come often in shiny suits and black glasses, asking almost the same question as you are asking now and it feels so strange that I have to answer them again. Of course, you have your badge and ID, but I can at the same time think those other ones had their badges but didn't want to show or something' The local Radio Shack guy said. He was a skinny guy that looked like he could be easily intimidated and I understood why he was afraid. The case was becoming quite sensitive and everyone didn't want to be too attached.

All other names and phone numbers in Neil's wallet were either disconnected or belonged to someone else. They might have been written in code of some sort, but we could never decode them. Even with I.G.'s expertise and connections, Neil's codes could never be broken or deciphered.

I eventually worked alone in Neil's apartment every day with the fire department helping with nothing but fresh scout air packs and bunker clothing. All I could think of was the case. When I close my eyes all I could see was the bloated dead body of who we **believed** to be Neil and sometimes the memory of his decomposing body bursting open. I drown myself in coffee and tried to stay awake for as many hours as possible just to connect all the dots that were apparent before us but still looked vague. I also wanted a clear I.D. that the body found was that of Don Neil. The possibility of a body switch stand-in was probable and possible. It could also account for the reason that the killers wrapped the face, and knowing that putrification would blot out any chance for fingerprints. I.G. and Jack had worked to find dental records, but the body was already buried and none were ever found. I wasn't one hundred percent sure who they buried in Bradford, Pennsylvania.

Sergeant Barker and other officers searched Neil's car, but just trash, magazines, and assorted electronic parts were found.

Then an idea about contacting Neil's ex-employer came and we tried it. My confidential informant tipped me about possible addresses and off I went with Sutgar in tow. We were shocked to receive a call sometimes later from a female caller that claimed to be acting in the interest of the FBI. They claimed they wanted all the pieces of evidence we had gathered because according to them they were all classified as Top Secret, EYES ONLY. It was at that point that we knew something was indeed fishy.

I went to one of the McDonnel Douglas buildings in Clear Lake City, near NASA where Neil was supposed to be working and met the security director, Ben Turner. Neil's space had been cleaned out, sterilized and there was no one around to interview. The security director stated that he thought that was Neil's workstation but couldn't be sure and didn't know who had cleaned the desks out and removed his computers and files. I knew there were cameras in the building due to the high security, however, when I asked for the film to be reviewed to ascertain who cleaned out Neil's desk he stated that the cameras were being repaired and he doubted there were any recent films. He stated that he would check, but later told me in a phone conversation that there was nothing on the tapes.

I asked him if he knew who called the apartment office to have them check on Neil and he stated that he didn't know if anyone had called. He referred me to call a woman I will call Betty, who was with McDonnell Douglas personnel department.

Calling her phone number took a while because first off, her number wasn't in Texas. I was worried I might not have our conversation well protected. I would have considered traveling to meet her but time was too short to arrange a meaningful meeting so I settled to speak more officially than interrogatively with Betty.

She was a soft-spoken woman when she answered my call. She sounded like a middle-aged woman that is rather not so excited speaking about Neil. She confirmed that Neil was an employee listed as an electronics engineer but his department and supervisor were blank. She could not tell me what building he worked at and did not have a record of his security clearances, or a photo of him on file. She stated that was very odd, but she stated that sometimes files are incomplete.

'I have never met him in person so I cannot speak of him in some certain way or describe him further than I have officer' Betty said when I asked her for more information. She stated that she had no further information. However, I was more than glad. Knowing Neil was an engineer explained a lot and validated why certain things were already adding up.

I.G. and Jack had confirmed that Ben was probably instructed what to say, and told that the cameras were not working.

Chapter Five: The Suspects

It was one of those cool evenings when I had time to chill over a bottle of beer with Sutgar that another snippet of good news came in. It was the evening of the twenty-second day of June 1983 and I was extremely tired. I had stopped at one of my hangouts and had a bag of peanuts almost cracked out. By now, Sutgar was in a conversation across the room that I was monitoring. There was soft country music playing in the background when a man walked to my table as slippery as imaginable.

'Straight Whiskey!' He said almost in a whisper to the bartender who replied to him with a nod. I cracked one more nut open and he knew that he had to say as much as he could before the bartender returned with his drink.

'I found his co-worker at McDonnel Douglas... You should see this...' He slipped a paper holder under my drink, said thanks to the bartender, and got his drinks and left my table. He had written all the information I needed.

Note: This man was never identified, and was not seen again around the Bay Area.

The name of the co-worker was Jack Williams who was a co-worker with Neil at McDonnel Douglas and stated that he knew Neil and had loaned him a Skripsit or Skripsi computer program on 51/4" disc, but Neil never returned it.

I had my leather briefcase with me containing pictures and a description of all the pieces of evidence gathered on the case. I opened to see if there was anywhere where we had a disk such as this one as evidence but there wasn't. I knew there wasn't but I needed to check. It was not found during the search of the apartment or his car.

I had Archie contact Jack Williams and set up a meeting at the King's Inn. Jack Williams met us and stated that he did not know what Neil was working on as Neil was very secretive, and he did not know where Neil had his office even though he had seen him a few times at the NASA café, and around the grounds on occasion. He sounded sure and very certain. He wasn't a man of many words and he sounded like he had a hammer in his hands, striking the nails in the right places. Jack Williams was a computer scientist at NASA and agreed to come to the apartment to help decipher the codes on computers. He stated that he was not afraid to help out as his position was highly visible and he had been through some other similar investigations previously. We told him we could offer some protection from anyone tailing him, etc. As a result of our meeting and his outward courage and apparent honesty, we invited him to go with us to Neil's apartment, which he eagerly accepted.

We drove divertingly to Neil's apartment around Noon, just in case there was a tail, but none was detected by Echoff, or Sutgar following separately. I was more enthusiastic about what he was going to do for the case than having a conversation with him. He walked into the crime scene and just like everyone, he couldn't help but whence at the smell, and macabre horror the apartment had taken on, even though most of the mess had been cleaned up.

'Most of the bad stuff had been moved out especially if we find them not to be of any use. Trust me, the room is in its best shape' Jack looked at me as he forced a smile. He settled on one of the computer desks and tried to put his fingers at work, trying to do all he could to crack the codes that seemed impossible. Just by the window was an antenna we had removed the second day of the original crime scene development and secured at the Webster P.D. property room. I had Archie and I.G. bring it in disguise so that if we were being surveilled they would not be connected with the investigation. They only appeared to be from ABC Clean and Cure Company out of Houston, Texas, which was a prop company we set up for the investigation. We brought it into the apartment in an oversized box with a dolly to throw off suspicion. I uncovered and placed it by one of Neil's computers and plugged it in just as Don Neil had it set up. It was so unusual looking that we felt Jack Williams would be in the best position to put it into good use. It looked nothing like any known technology existing; very futuristic, though crudely assembled.

Sadly, Jack Williams couldn't figure the codes on the computer, and also stated that the curious antenna was perhaps something Neil had invented to communicate with through his Hamm Radio but he didn't know how it worked. His best guess was that Don had found a way to contact a satellite and clear a password to connect and transmit.

'For me not to be able to do much with these codes, it definitely must be one hell of a code and this antenna... perhaps you should talk to Connie Walker. He is also an engineer they had the same NASA connection and I have always known they didn't get along; you know?' Jack Williams said.

'Who is this Connie Walker? Any information at this point will go a long way. Please help Neil, Jack' I said, trying to be more personal than inquisitorial. Jack Williams looked at me with eyes that suggested he knew what I was up to. He packed his bags and was ready to leave the room. When he got to the door he turned and shook his head almost apologetically.

'I am sorry I couldn't be of help. Maybe you should talk to people at NASA. Maybe they would tell you about this Connie Walker and things that may be very beneficial' Jack said. We left by a different route and all at differing times. I arranged for Jack Williams and his wife to be put up for a few nights out of town so that we could cool his link to the investigation.

Archie found a C.I. at NASA who confirmed the engineer's name and location. He also stated that he had told him that he was glad Neil was out of the way as it left him in line to get a promotion. I found the engineer and met with him at his house in Clear Lake city. Tailed there by two men in a small car. Deputy Echoff was in a cool car and watched them for activities.

The case was hitting the climax and I needed to be careful. Clear Lake had a coordinated ambiance like everyone was monitoring everyone; like everything was under definite surveillance. The two men who drove behind me were back a few paces away smoking their cigarette. I hesitated to get out of my vehicle for a while but eventually did. I had barely knocked when he opened and waved me in.

'Everything you said sounded strange. I wasn't in any sort of competition with him and even though he wasn't my friend, he wasn't my enemy. We had a healthy competition expected from co-workers which is essential for every workplace to grow... sorry for my bad manners, do you want anything?' He dazzled me with words and even though I was half-listening, I was studying the room. It looked too prepared to be real. It was as though everything was carefully and particularly placed; something most homes didn't have.

'No I don't. thanks!' I said as he went on and on, denying having made any such comments and stated that he and Neil had had words and that he was going to get a promotion that would've been Neil's.

'Tell me about this project. It seems to be the only thing that is currently tying every clue together that we still do not have an answer to.' I said.

'No, I basically cannot talk about that... I am so sorry. They are all classified information and I cannot indulge any of these details' He said without blinking like he had rehearsed everything he wanted to say to me. He continued saying some of the information is proprietary and could open him to several legal liabilities and it was at that point I knew we weren't the only person in the room. I was under surveillance, we were being watched and listened to. I had no choice to shake all tails off and head back toward the Webster PD station.

Deputy Echoff called me on the radio and asked me to meet him at Carlos' Beer Garden. He felt he had spooked the tail, and we could meet up there. I was going to head straight to my desk at the Webster P.D. but I remembered everything I needed to do was scattered in town and I wouldn't achieve much on my office desk. I had Deputy Echoff meet me at Carlos's Beer Garden right out the back door of the P.D. and in the dark alley. I snuck out and left with him in his car, out of the prying eyes.

Even though I knew to go to the crime scene was no longer safe, the apartment had created some kind of longing in me. It was almost the case that I couldn't do much unless I was in it.

I was back in the apartment, coffee in hand, pencil behind my ear, pacing around the room and drawing my fingers across the table when I found the name of a man and a phone number that did work, sketched almost illegibly on a scrap of paper. I quickly headed to Days Inn to make the call.

When I called, the man was a private pilot who lived in New York and had met Don Neil at a small airport in Texas and found that he was a Hamm Radio operator as well and they communicated many times for a few years over Hamm.

There was that black taped, mysterious box from Neil's window that so much attention had not been drawn to, but which I was drawn to as soon as I heard the pilot talking about Hamm radio conversations. Almost apparently the black box on the window was a homemade satellite link as Neil had no other wired to his Hamm radio and no tower that would aid him in boosting his signal that far. This man stated that they talked about flying and electronics, as well as Neil's attempts to locate his daughter.

I got nothing else from the pilot and I seemed contented because every new person I got to talk to about Neil had one new thing or the other to talk about him. With all that I had gathered, I strongly felt there were so many things left still untapped. The apartment became a treasure hunt site and we needed all the treasures that we could get insofar as they would get us to the bottom of the case. We had diskettes that couldn't be decoded which were swapped back to me and tagged as evidence and we went mad basically because we knew there was something somewhere we weren't looking at.

On the eleventh day of July 1983, the unfortunate thing happened. Boxing began and the final sweep of the crime scene commenced. This was the same room that had homed me almost throughout those moments that I needed a good space to think about the emerging facts of the case that was before me. Everywhere was ripped apart while conducting the final sweep. The carpets were torn open, the walls were ripped out, the car was turned in and out just for that one strand of evidence that might put an end to our misery, and offer a solid clue.

The most astonishing of all these things that were beginning to happen was that no one contacted us aside from those we reached. For a middle-aged man like Donald Neil, who according to people we have spoken to, had worked really hard in the organization that employed him, it was just a matter of sympathy for the organization to reach out, to speak well about his service, to commend him as some sort of last words in commensuration of the deceased's existence. It never happened. It was if Neil never did work with them. It was as though; he wasn't even missed at all. Their silence perhaps gave a clue about how desperately they wanted him out of their way and if I chose to disbelieve this, that would be a result of a conscious effort from them to make me believe in the negative; they never did.

No intel group contacted us as well, no Feds, it was just the naïve police department doing all the work for justice. I was walking a tightrope I was well familiar with as I had set up and worked both sides of the silent fence before. Jack Blaine had warned me previously of a shadow investigation which they could not afford to have exposed. I reminded myself of that frequently throughout the process and certainly did not want to jeopardize whatever it was that they were working. This time the chessboard was rigged in the advantage of whoever was controlling the publicity, and I knew better than to try to find out who, and I knew better than to cross the line they were drawing in the sand. If I got too close to the wire or stepped over the boundaries of their expectations they would launch their plan to shut down the publicity. That meant coming straight at me, and the department. If it were me assigned on the other side of the chessboard, I would launch a campaign to discredit the investigation and have the FBI move in to take over the investigation. That would be a sure way to control the outcome, and bring the investigation to a halt. These are tedious games that are played for all the marbles.

Just across the road, while we were doing our last sweep for evidence, I noted two men in a car watching from Mario's Pizza across the street. Echoff down the street was keeping them under surveillance. When Echoff drove up on them they drove away and headed down I-45 toward Houston at high speed. Echoff lost them in traffic and there were no Houston P.D. units available to stop them for ID.

We were beginning to come to terms with our misery when Barker raised an alarm that gave us fresh hope. He had found the details of a bank account affirming Neil's annual pay and connecting those payments to his silent employer. There was a new trail to follow, a new lead to pursue. Sutgar was the man for the challenge and he got to work right away. It was not long before he and I.G. had run across two fake accounts and were tracking several more. Deputy Echoff helped out with the footwork and visited the banks with subpoenas. The accounts were dry of funds as of several months before the murder. It indicated that withdrawals had been made by Don Neil. Sutgar and I.G. located one of the banks that had surveillance footage that corresponded to one of the days of withdrawal, however, Don Neil was not on the tapes.

****

Donald Neil was married and he had a beautiful daughter. Some sort of rift came between them and this led to their divorce. Unfortunately, Neil's wife had the custody of their only daughter whom Neil loved all his life and did all he could to reconnect back with. Betty was his ex-wife's name and she was remarried to a high profile medical professional. She hated Neil and wouldn't let him deal directly with their daughter. She was certainly one of the most important people I needed to talk to and when Neil's brother obliged me with her contact, I immediately put a call through.

Talking with her made me see some other side of Donald Neil that was perhaps in the dark until the conversation. Neil had hired private investigators and others to trace her every move. When I remarked that he didn't have enough money to do that, she stated that he did contract intel work and that they paid him very well in separate accounts that were in different names, some individual and some fraudulent company names.

Betty's description of Neil's private life was almost expository. According to her, Neil was a pervert and made her go to strip clubs and watch the girls with him. She described his violent temper and how greatly stressed he was since he left Bell Helicopter where he was a design engineer and did the laser sighting device for Helo gunships, and other work that he couldn't discuss. She stated that she thought he was working for NASA on a top-secret project after that and moved to Webster. He became very secretive after that and bitter. I made several phone calls to her throughout the investigation, and she made it very clear that Don was relentless to get his daughter back and harassed them constantly.

'You know; I am glad that he's dead. I am so sorry to say it but I sincerely am!' She said. I asked her if she had anything to do with it or knew anything about it. She denied taking any part and stated that until I called her, she did not know that he was dead.

Coming back from Betty's fancy home was a combination of stress and unresolved questions. I never wanted to know what it felt like to have a daughter and be deprived of her presence in my life. I never wanted to know what it felt like to lose a woman as nice as Betty. It was in the middle of my thought that I remembered the bloody wallet and what I could do with it.

I went to Houston PD Lieutenant Boulet and Sergeant Bracken of the Harris County Sheriff's Office where they had the first new laser, as they had the only law enforcement building in Houston that had a water main big enough to cool the laser. I asked to test the laser on a bloody fingerprint on the wallet. They agreed. Excitedly, I called Officer Collett at HPD crime analysis to complete a run up on Neil and everything needed to bring a reasonable clue but nothing was found. The laser enhanced the print but the photography didn't get a good enough record of the print.

I consulted with Bill Temple a Houston PD computer fingerprint analyst. They had a new electronic computer room for latent prints that were just coming into limited use. They offered to look at the bloody print and I jumped at the invitation. Unfortunately, they could not develop the print well enough to type or ID. This was 1983, a year of many patent designs and nuances for law enforcement and forensic science, none of which revealed any evidentiary usefulness in this case.

Chapter Six: The Psychic

As we were at dead ends, the Webster Chief stated that there was a class he attended at the FBI National Academy in psychic investigation. There was this Psychic lady that came to teach about these types of investigations. He stated that he still had her contact and thought she was not only really good, but it was at least worth a try. At this point, I wanted to explore everything possible. The psychic was Mary-Linda, quite popular at that time, and I was willing to take my investigation to her. I reached out to her.

She needed a point of contact with the victim and the wallet was readily available. I sent it to her and she was more than willing to help. The wallet was mysteriously intercepted by an unknown person or agency in the mail to Mary-Linda as the seal was broken. I had put a red thread in the wallet to ID it, and the thread was missing. Mary-Linda didn't get the wallet until the eighteenth of July but when she eventually did, the vague story of whatever had happened that night became more meaningful. Mary-Linda gave first reading over the phone from Virginia with her assistant present. Barker and I listened as she gave the details about how Neil was murdered, and where he lived. She gave the name of our first suspect, one Raul whom we put Jack Blaine, I.G. and Archie on right away to try to locate and trail.

In my years as a police officer, I have come to notice that all seems well when you have a known suspect, as against when you are working on just clues. There is this vague satisfaction that accompanies it; a feeling of fulfillment that you are on the right path. That feeling is very slippery because it may get you unfocused. You are distracted by the idea of a suspect that you may not be focused on other pieces of evidence that might just be right under your nose until it is too late.

I had my suspicions and even though it was gotten through a psychic, the admissibility of which I wasn't so sure if contested in a court of law, I was glad I had something to glue all of my pieces of evidence and clues on. The most exciting of this was, with Mary-Linda I didn't have to do much. I didn't have to travel down to consult her, I didn't have to tear down walls and carpet to get anything. It was a phone conversation that yielded so many potentials.

Perhaps I would have disbelieved if I had given Mary-Linda any form of briefing. I only needed to send a wallet, and then test that she was truly and factually connected with the case and could offer answers that we didn't have. I had no reason but to trust her.

On the twenty-eighth day of July 1983, we had a local police sketch artist sit in on a phone call with Mary-Linda and sketched Raul. Mary-Linda had Neil's wallet to hold in her hand at this reading and gave details about the Night Owl Club and how Neil frequented it. She gave us the general location around a large airport, which turned out to be William P. Hobby Airport in Houston, Texas on Telephone road.

Journeying to a precise location with a name in mind could reveal some additional clues, and we surely needed some. We were focused on one thing; The Night Owl. Sutgar ironically located the only club with the name, "Night Owl" in the Houston area, and it was right down Telephone Road, just a few miles from the W.P. Hobby Airport, giving us more reason to believe our inestimable psychic.

During her reading, Mary-Linda described a blonde-haired man who fit the description of John, and she said that he was with Raul in Neil's booth with red tufted leather, the only booth in the place. I imagined her saying those words. I hadn't seen so many psychics in my life and my mind drifted to the darkest of things. I imagined she wrapped her hair up when it was time to do what she did. I imagined her eyes rolled up and smoke oozing out of the ambiance that surrounded her. It was a terrible imagination I had to snap out to embrace a better one. Time travel.

I Imagined Mary-Linda tracking all that Neil might have done. I had touched the Wallet, so perhaps I was in the story. Maybe I was drifting after one of the crime scenes I successfully followed through. This pattern of thoughts was nice to imagine but I had to once again abandon it because I knew it was all speculation.

In her moment of connecting with the unknown, traveling back in time, she saw a clock on the end of the bar by the restrooms, an electronic dart game, and stated that when I found the bar I would find it was not the type of establishment that I thought it would be. She further stated that the men she saw in the booth with Neil could've been planning Neil's death, with his approval. Perhaps he wanted his daughter to feel sorry for him and wanted to reward his brother with the insurance policy, etc. Also, he could've been planning the death of a stand-in for Neil, and how they could cover it up. Mary-Linda offered many scenarios, all of which had some thread of logic or possibility based on what we knew.

To corroborate Mary-Linda's story was amazing, but many of her statements were verified as Sutgar, Jack Blaine, and I arrived at the Night Owl Club. The parking lot was exactly as Mary-Linda had described, even the giant pothole out front. The bar was longer than it was wide, and there was a clock at the end of the bar over the restroom hallway. An electronic dart game was to our left, and only one booth existed that was red tufted leather. We were all looking in amazement at each other as this was a little unnerving.

I had assembled three photo lineups with Don Neil's picture in only one of them. I introduced myself to the owner and showed him my I.D. I explained that I wanted to show him a series of photos and see if he knew anyone. I explained before he looked at them that this was not to identify a suspect, but to see if they knew a person whom we had been told frequented the bar. I asked all the others to not look to preserve the integrity of their answers. As I laid out the 18 photos the owner quickly pointed to Don Neil and stated, 'Oh my God, I hope Mr. Neil is not in trouble', as he pointed straight to his photo without any hesitation, or doubt. I then showed the owner's wife, and two female waitresses the same lineup, but separate of each other. Each one of them had a shocked look of concern but picked out Don Neil easily and quickly. They all confirmed that Neil was a frequent visitor and that he always wore his suit with his NASA badges, and pocket protector. They went on to state that Neil had begun meeting with a blonde-haired gentleman within the last year as well as a Hispanic man and that they always sat in the red tufted leather booth. They all described them as friendly, but very secretive, and they always thought that the blonde-haired man and the Hispanic man were coercing Neil. They were afraid of the two, although they never started any trouble.

Also as the psychic stated, I was surprised to find that the Night Owl was privately and family-owned, and although in a very rough part of town was a friendly bar with some local old-timers as regulars. It did not fit the stereotype of the typical bar in that area. Mary-Linda's predictions had hit a home run this time, and unbelievably corroborated! We all left there very astounded, but glad that something had been learned and corroborated.

The Night Owl Club was located through the right-hand doorway at the time of the murder

It was around seven in the morning when I got a call from the Webster P.D. dispatcher that I had a package. It was the FBI and they had dropped off a set of Neil's fingerprints for me that I had requested. I looked in the manila envelope and there were two sets of FBI ten-print cards with Don Neil's name as if they were his fingerprints on them. I noticed that they were copies right away, and not very good ones.

I asked the dispatcher who the man was that dropped these off, and if he left a card. She stated that he came in when patrol was working on a major accident and she did not get to talk to him except that he said he was with the FBI, but showed no ID.

'Can you describe him for me please?' I said, urging her reluctant face with a smile. She took a deep breath as though she had seen a monster and was summing up all the courage to describe that which she had seen.

'He's white, a tall white man of about... probably five feet eleven. From his look, I think he is definitely in his mid-twenties. He had a dark suit on and matching sunglasses. That is all I can say about him... I think I should get going. I have a lot of delivery to do today' She said.

I took the suspicious ten-print cards to Houston Police Department fingerprint section again to enhance, but they could not use them as the quality was too poor. We did smoke the manila envelope in the lab with Ninhydrin, but no usable prints were discovered. I called the Houston FBI office and asked if they knew who dropped off the ten-print cards and after checking through their office, they stated that they didn't know.

It was around three in the morning when one of my confidential informants who was living just across the driveway of Neil's apartment called me to inform me that lights were on at Neil's apartment and men in suits were ransacking it.

That was all the prompt I needed to get the ball rolling. I was desperate to catch even one of them. I immediately called Webster P.D. dispatch and had them send patrol units to the scene to cordon the area. On my instruction, everyone would be held until my arrival. I left my residence to check by and realized very quickly that I was being followed.

I sped up and shook the tail close to Clover Field Airport in Friendswood, Texas and went to Neil's apartment. The seal on the door was broken, and I found computers thrown on the floor and diskettes scattered. Two computers were missing. Neil's lamp was turned on, and another lamp was left at the scene that was not there previously.

I took the lamp that was left into custody and sealed the apartment back. I asked patrol to keep a special watch for the remainder of the night. I tried dusting the lamp for prints, but the surface was rough and no prints could be found or lifted. I talked to the confidential informant that had witnessed the men ransacking Neil's apartment via phone the next day, but she could not offer any other information except that she thought that they had a radio in their hand, and when the dispatch call went out for units to go to Neil's apartment, they quickly left. She did not see any vehicles in the area, or anyone leaving the complex on foot. The CI had a police scanner and was listening to all traffic.

****

The FBI seemed not to be interested in our case, and I recalled Jack Blaine stating previously that they were working a close shadow investigation and did not want to overtly be involved. But everywhere I went, the story seemed not to be the same. They were everywhere we weren't and there was never a time they affirmed anything about Neil's case. I had called them several times to inquire at the Houston FBI office about the grey areas around Neil's case but each time, they denied ever knowing anything or being interested in anything.

During my course of the investigation and speaking with Mary-Linda, my list of suspects I began to grow became three. They were all connected to Neil's death in many ways I found it difficult to understand and I was willing to know. I had my confidential informants and assets everywhere. They were my eyes and ears, looking out and watching to make sure I had all the information I needed. It was a relief when one of them called to inform me that these three men had gone to the local clubs where NASA employees frequented about satellite technology, SDI, and stated that they were working on such projects.

There was John, as described by Mary-Linda. His description matched an east German contract agent for KGB that we were working on. He was blonde and was aged between twenty-five to thirty and about six feet tall. There was Bob of the same KGB who was dark-haired, a bit taller than John at about six feet and two inches tall. He was a bit older too as he was between the age of thirty to thirty-five years old. The last on the list was Darren, a six feet tall all business guy. They were all without any detectible accent, no scars, marks, or tattoos, but Darren did wear black-rimmed glasses.

The body needs the eyes and ears but also needs the legs and hands to function. My ears and hands were scattered across many agencies and assets, one of them was Jack Blaine. He was my long-time family friend and covert controller. He was my extended legs in those moments I needed to stretch more than I really could do. Two of the men who I had trailed as connected to the crime and who were asking questions too were confirmed by Jack to be KGB agents while one of them was known by Sutgar as an East German contract agent.

I knew them through my other investigations and had CI's watching them previously. According to the CI's they had all left town after Neil's murder, and they had not seen them again. The East German fit the description given by Edna, and the witnesses at the Night Owl but I had no photos to show them and no way to ID any of them.

A CI stated that Kent Mabry had Neil's 22 rifle that he stole from him and that Kent was in the hospital with an eye injury. Barker checked the story out and Mabry denied any rifle, and none was found in his possession. Barker checked his parents' house but found nothing.

I showed photos line-up with Mabry in it to Edna, but she did not pick him, or anyone else in the lineup out as the man she had seen enter Neil's apt around the time of the murder. She had never seen Mabry before.

It was not until the third of August 1983, that the sketched portrait of Raul was released on the official Texas Crime Analysis Bulletin as a suspect for murder. The portrait was done through a call with Mary-Linda and her assistant and the artist at my office drawing as Mary-Linda guided her.

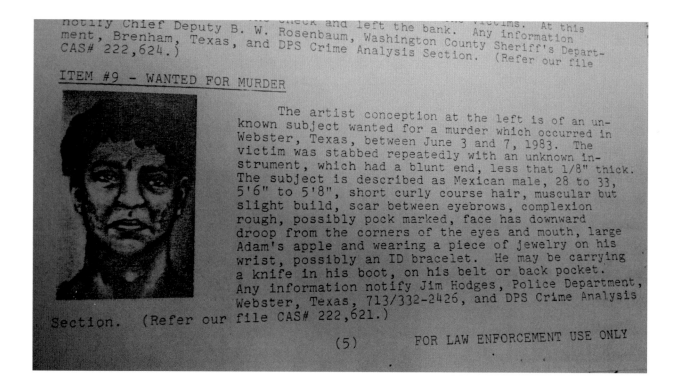

notify Chief Deputy B. W. Rosenbaum, Washington County Sheriff's Department, Brenham, Texas, and DPS Crime Analysis Section. (Refer our file CAS# 222,624.)

ITEM #9 - WANTED FOR MURDER

The artist conception at the left is of an unknown subject wanted for a murder which occurred in Webster, Texas, between June 3 and 7, 1983. The victim was stabbed repeatedly with an unknown instrument, which had a blunt end, less that 1/8" thick. The subject is described as Mexican male, 28 to 33, 5'6" to 5'8", short curly course hair, muscular but slight build, scar between eyebrows, complexion rough, possibly pock marked, face has downward droop from the corners of the eyes and mouth, large Adam's apple and wearing a piece of jewelry on his wrist, possibly an ID bracelet. He may be carrying a knife in his boot, on his belt or back pocket. Any information notify Jim Hodges, Police Department, Webster, Texas, 713/332-2426, and DPS Crime Analysis Section. (Refer our file CAS# 222,621.)

(5)   FOR LAW ENFORCEMENT USE ONLY

Bulletin I created and sent to the Texas Dept. of Public Safety for law enforcement publication only.

I also contacted two of the Houston TV stations as well as the Houston Chronicle for their assistance in broadcasting this information and asking for assistance from anyone who may have a lead on the crime. All of them informed me that they had been told by the local FBI office not to broadcast anything to the public as this was a very sensitive and controlled investigation that "They" were working. Publicity was squelched. I again called the Houston FBI office but they denied having any such conversations with the news media at all about this case.

Chapter Seven: Endless Tunnel

Neil's case had become a labyrinth. It had a clustered structure of infinite pieces of evidence, an assortment of people involved, and a rough path that cannot easily be scaled through. Many endless chases went on and on with many confidential informants bringing on leads that led to nowhere basically because they had been compromised. There was a suspect that seemed unreal and untraceable and there were suspects that were already on the run. There were FBI agents on our tails and those who claimed to be FBI but who the bureau would always deny having anything to do with them.

Mary-Linda was the only green light and we were determined to shine her on our path until feasible results were achieved. Neil's brother seemed to be the only relative that cared much about the deceased and aside both of us, no one seemed to care; not his ex-wife and daughter, not the government and not his employer. It was as though everyone surrounding him or that knew how well he existed wanted him out of their way.

Neil's brother agreed to pay for Mary-Linda to fly to Houston, Texas to meet with us as a follow-up and to get her more engaged with the crime. She stayed in Houston for four days and in those four days, I had my chance to prove all my imaginations wrong. She was a very nice and grounded woman who carried herself with the aura of grace like she knew exactly what she was doing. A real professional.

The first day we took her to Webster PD for briefing, and then to Neil's apartment where she showed me that truly, she knew what she was doing. She went to the exact spot where his body was found and laid down exactly as his body was positioned on the floor.

There was no way she would've had prior knowledge of this as only Barker and I were in the apartment and saw, or handled the body. It was a revelation so pure, so true that once again, the invigorating chase after justice for Neil was reborn. There seemed to be substance whenever Mary-Linda was involved and substance was all that we needed.

For the next days to come, she became ill and had to walk out of the apartment several times to get her breath and regroup her thoughts. She was able to give her impressions further that Raul played a part in the murder, and knew Neil through the blonde-headed man from the Night Owl Club. We drove her around the area and found that Clover Field Airport (Now, City of Pearland, Texas Municipal Airport) was the airport she had seen in her vision where Raul and the blonde-haired man went after the murder and flew a light plane out.

It was August of the year Donald Neil died and there had not been a single local or national news item about a cold blood murder that had occurred in Texas. The criminal analysis bulletin wasn't doing much either and so I was glad when another entrance opened in the case's labyrinth.

I was contacted by Capt. Garcia of the US Border Patrol as he was running raids then on construction sites where illegal aliens were working in the Clear Lake area. He was eager to help me in taking the case a bit further amidst the Hispanic folks. He was willing to discuss the case more with me over dinner as well as help in circulating the fliers that had declared Raul wanted. He sounded so enthusiastic about helping and I fell for it.

I met him in the field the first time we met, he had taken the fliers from me and circulated it almost at once.

'I just want to help' he said to me with a smile as he led me into his house. That was when I knew something was wrong in every way. Everything seemed not to be right, everything seemed strange. The apartment looked staged and lacked any noise from a TV or stereo. I felt I was being recorded remotely so I guarded everything I said. 'Don't you ever think you might be in danger… that your life might be at risk? Why are you ever this relentless about a man you never knew, that you never met?' I have been asked these questions so many times and I have asked myself those questions so many times but each time, two words came flashing across my mind; the truth. I just wanted to know the truth, the exact truth about what had happened and if justice can be achieved through this truth. I just wanted to see the bottom of that endless tunnel.

Neil's case made me flashback to my training in covert operations many years ago before and after my tour in the Vietnam War. It was during one of the flashbacks that I recalled how to dodge the Garcias' visit and questions, and how I could find out about them. I called Jack Blaine and met with him to hear the information his assets had run down. It was discovered that his wife was an FBI field agent but she never stated that to me. We had dined together, talked together, and joked about how the FBI was naturally killing the case and it was only natural and expected of her to mention that she was one of them – but she didn't. Garcia never called me with a lead after that at all, which was unusual. In the vast number of Hispanic males in the Houston – Galveston, there should have been at least one lead, even if it wasn't the suspect, Raul.

Again, another hope was ditched and I went back to my bar. I had so many let-downs trapped in my system and I needed to unwind. I could remember sitting down scrolling through the many pages of my documented pieces of evidence, looking to see if there was any loophole left but there was nothing. With just a little help aside from that Mary-Linda had done for us, we could have pulled through but there was no help except a determined mind.

I spoke to Neil's wife more often and I garnered more information that made me start coming into certain conclusions. She hated Neil with every breath in her and all her description of Neil was tainted with it. I had no evidence to consider her a suspect. I believed her sincerity, and that couldn't be ignored.

My Last Reflections

For more than thirty-six years, this case had been on and off a few desks of other detectives, along with a few of those that knew the genesis of this case with me. I am now left alone to tell the inconclusive tale of espionage, murder, and cover-up of an unfortunate event without an appropriate ending.

Chief of Police Jerry Barker died a mysterious death from pneumonia complications a few years after I left WPD. John Eckhoff died of the same anomaly a year before the publishing of this book. I had just talked to him on a Friday about finishing the book and we had planned to meet the first of the following week. I texted John on Monday to arrange the meeting and received a shocking answer from his wife, stating that he had died over the weekend due to pneumonia. Archie Fletcher was shot to death in a staged robbery in Bolivia in 1991. No suspects were ever identified or arrested. I.G. Blackmon disappeared during the Afghan invasion in 2001. He was assumed dead several years later. Jack Blaine died an old man after our symbolic meeting at President Lyndon B. Johnson's Ranch in Stonewall, Texas. Silently, and swiftly, just as they lived.

I left the WPD with a few conclusions. One remote possibility was that the murder had been orchestrated by Neil's ex-wife due to strong hatred. There was also the possibility that Neil himself had designed his death so that his daughter would feel sorry for him and his brother would get the insurance money. Another planning scenario that Neil could've followed is using a stand-in to be killed in his place. This would cause the daughter to feel sorry for him, his brother to get the insurance money, and Neil to retire somewhere to start over in a new life. Or, more probably, that he was killed by the foreign agents in the last-ditch torture for information on SDI, and that he was killed either by accident or on purpose as they had reached their last option. We confirmed that after they had lived in the Bay Area for many years, they all three left the Houston-Galveston area right after the murder. The only other rational answer is a haphazard killing due to Neil's affiliation with the Hispanic girl who came to his apartment from time-to-time. The coincidental paths of Don Neil and some bad friends, or a jealous boyfriend of the girl that happened upon him to rob or steal from him. The entire nature of this method of murder and torture are only revealed in part so that the investigation is protected.

I left the Webster Police Department as I was invited to bring my covert tricks to the City of Pearland, Texas Police Department by then chief, Glen Stanford. In my 51st year of public service, I still continue to serve in various ways.

The files missing from the case report: These included a multitude of photographs, the hand notes and sketches, as well as the typed version of the case reports, other officer's entries after I left WPD, any case activity after my last entry 09-19-1983, Psychic reports, Composite sketch, five computers, two oscilloscopes, Hamm Radio, mystery antennae device with windowpane still attached, computer discs both 2 ¼ and 51/2" diskettes.

The lab reports, Neil's wallet, coded sheets print outs of codes, fraudulent ten-print cards with Don Neil's name on them and everything that we have ever worked on, taken away as though they never existed. But they forgot to take one of the most important things; my voice.

Not only must Justice be done; it also must be seen to have been done. And even though I had my conclusion about this case, in the U.S. law there is no statute of limitations on murder.

The case is still open, and still active, and maybe the answer is out there somewhere. The truth may still surface if given the room to breathe. I have vowed to assist the Webster P.D. and any other law enforcement agency to solve this crime. Although I have changed names and information in this report to protect those involved, I have provided the detectives of the Webster P.D. with the real names and all of the actual in-depth information that I have so that they may carry on.

I did learn that after my 2015 visit to the Webster P.D. that their cold case detectives analyzed the few items left in the property room for a chance of DNA and other advanced forensic procedures that were not available at the time of the murder. Sadly, no new evidence was found.

Perhaps you have discovered the keys and puzzles I have left in this true roman a clef. I still work this case many nights in my dreams and many days in my daydreams. I drive to the murder scene, or drive by other locations that we visited during the investigation, and stop and walk around still wondering, still looking. I owe that to Don Neil and I owe it to society. I proudly stand by my oath as a law enforcement officer, and I never

give up on a case.

"Don't become a mere recorder of facts, but try to penetrate the mystery of their origin." ~ Ivan Pavlov